DOGFISH
and the Gift of Inclusion

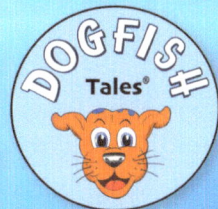

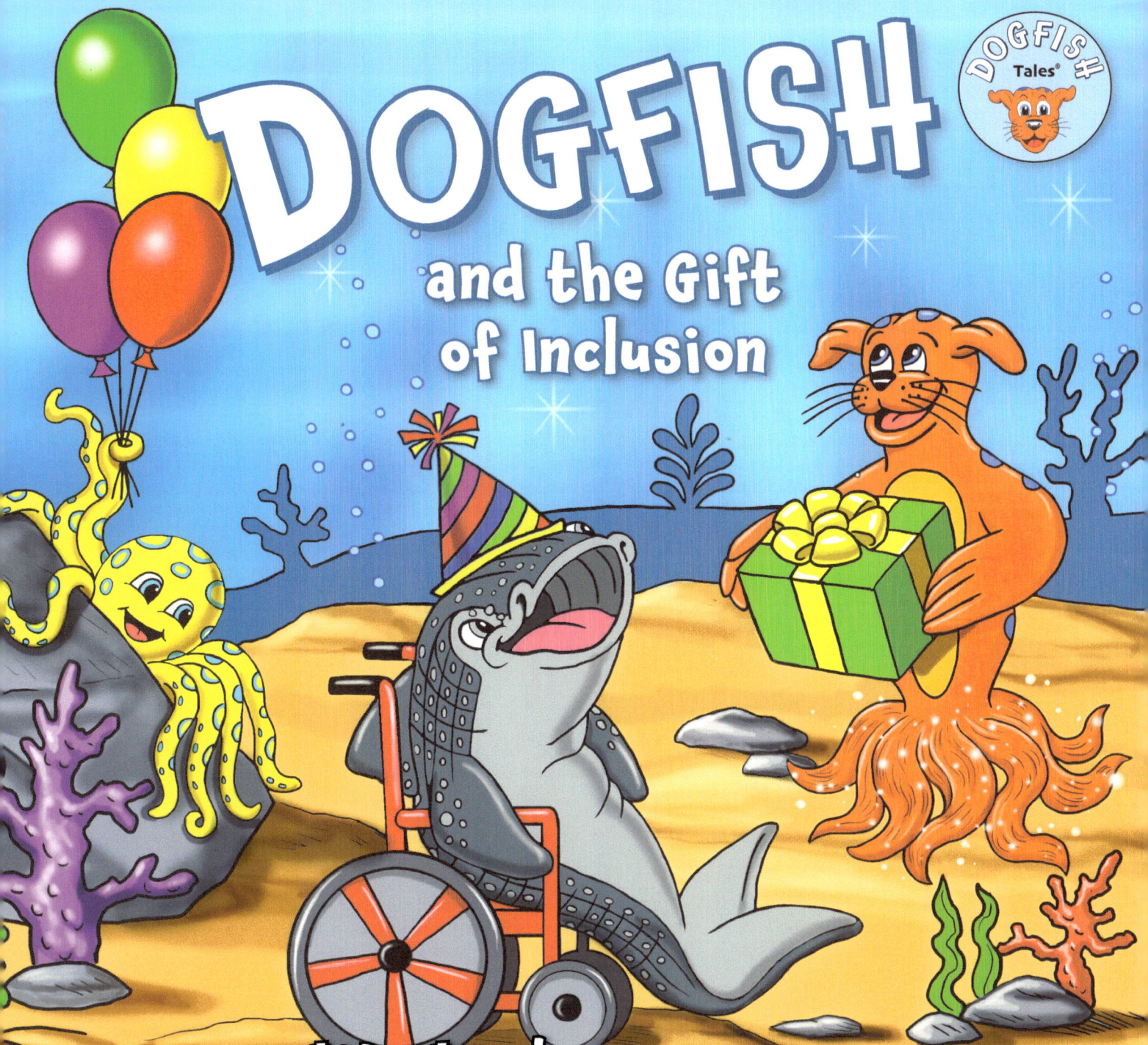

DOGFISH Tales®

WRITTEN BY **Rita Reed** ILLUSTRATED BY **Craig Cartwright**

Dogfish and the Gift of Inclusion
Published by Fine Eye Media
Thousand Oaks, CA

Names: Reed, Rita, author. | Cartwright, Craig, illustrator.
Title: Dogfish and the gift of inclusion / written by Rita Reed ; illustrated by Craig Cartwright.
Description: Thousand Oaks, CA : Fine Eye Media, [2024] | Series: Dogfish tales. | Audience: Juvenile. | Summary: Dogfish and friends receive an invitation to celebrate Wally the Whale Shark's birthday in Mexico! But when Ollie goes missing, it's all fins and flippers on deck to find him, because the party can't start unless EVERYONE is included!--Publisher.
Identifiers: ISBN: 978-1-7357862-6-1 (paperback) | 978-1-7357862-7-8 (hardcover)
Subjects: LCSH: Dogfish--Juvenile fiction. | Whale shark--Juvenile fiction. | Birthday parties--Juvenile fiction. | Friendship--Juvenile fiction. | Social integration--Juvenile fiction. | Cultural pluralism--Juvenile fiction. | Marine animals--Juvenile fiction. | Mexico--Juvenile fiction. | CYAC: Dogfish--Fiction. | Whale shark--Fiction. | Birthday parties--Fiction. | Friendship-- Fiction. | Social acceptance--Fiction. | Cultural pluralism--Fiction. | Marine animals--Fiction. | Mexico--Fiction. | BISAC: JUVENILE FICTION / Diversity & Multicultural. | JUVENILE FICTION / Disabilities. | JUVENILE FICTION / Social Themes / Friendship.
Classification: LCC: PZ7.1.R431 D642 2024 | DDC: [Fic]--dc23

Cover and Interior design by Victoria Wolf, wolfdesignandmarketing.com. Copyright owned by Rita Reed.

Illustrations by Craig Cartwright.

QUANTITY PURCHASES: Schools, companies, professional groups, clubs, and other organizations may qualify for special terms when ordering quantities of this title. For information, email Rita@FineEyeMedia.com

FINEEYEMEDIA

To my daughter, Rachel.

You are truly my angel on earth.

Thank you to all the individuals who work tirelessly to spread the message of disability inclusion. I would especially like to thank these two beautiful souls who have encouraged me to write this story: Jannesy DeLeon and Rebecca Rubin Seligson.

Peeking out the window Dogfish rubbed his sleepy eyes as the mailman delivered a **VERY BIG SURPRISE!**

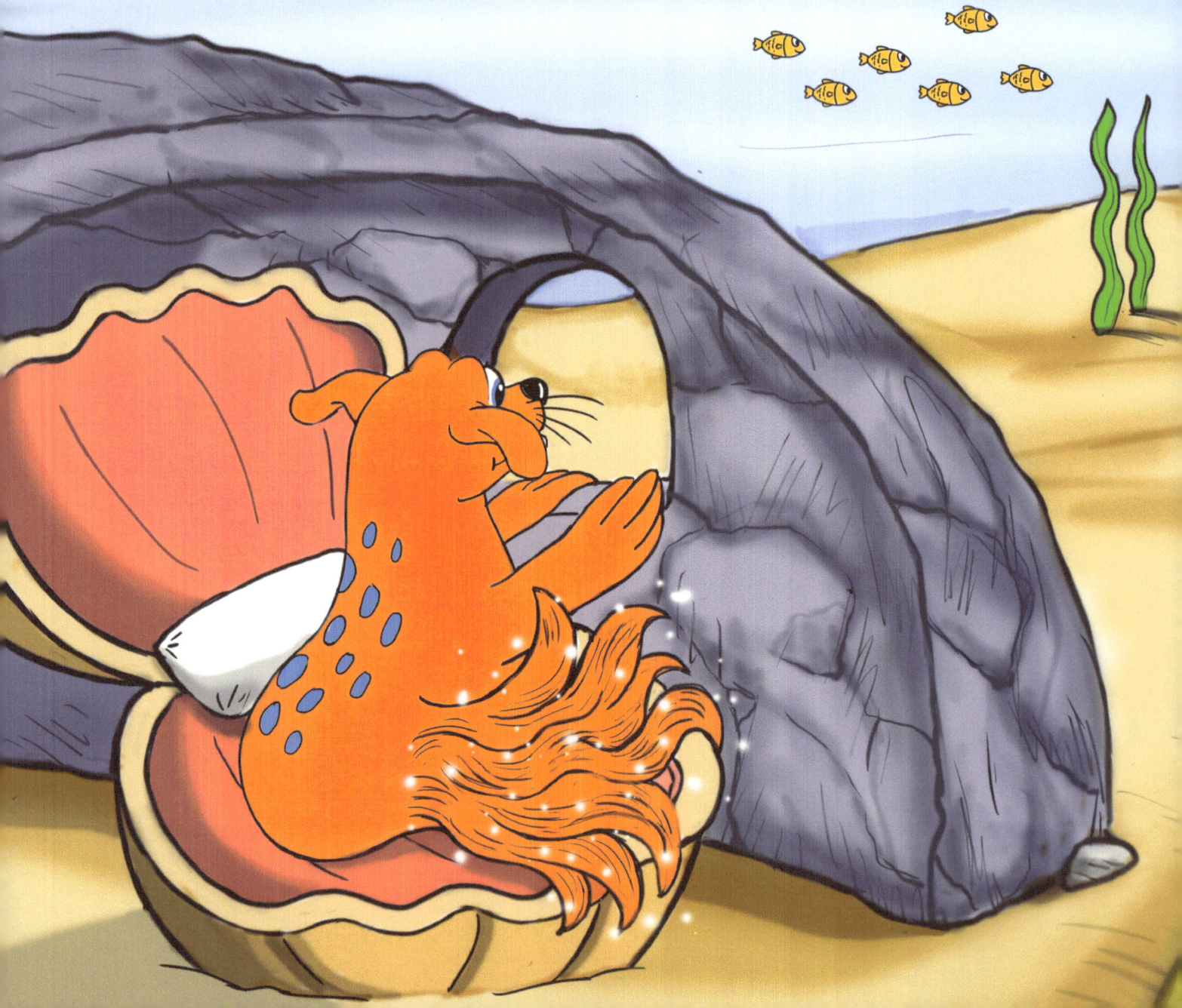

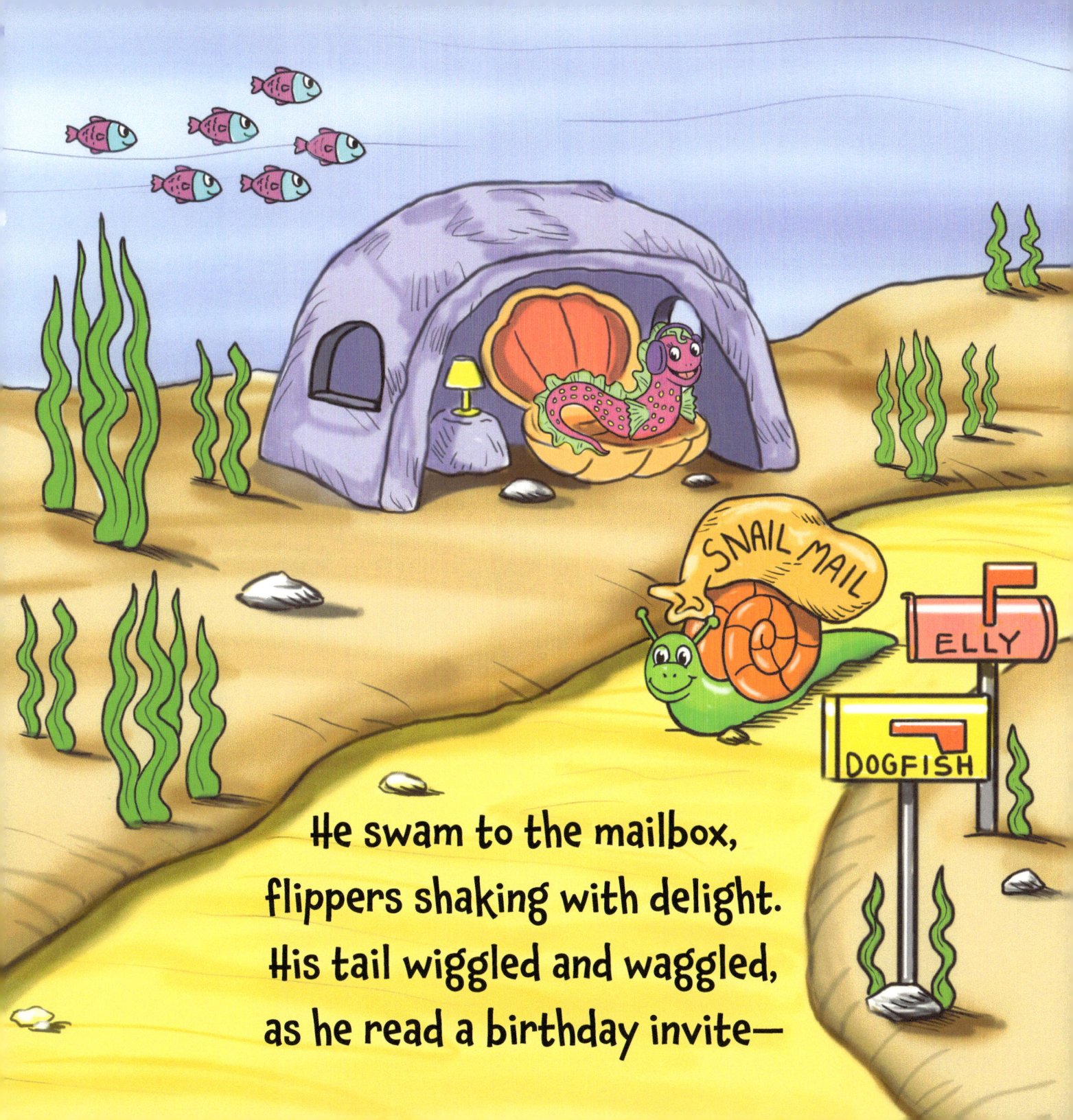

He swam to the mailbox,
flippers shaking with delight.
His tail wiggled and waggled,
as he read a birthday invite—

Join us for a party a short swim away to Los Cabos, Mexico It's time to celebrate!

Wally the Whale Shark is having a BIRTHDAY!

We'll be at Coral Park 2 p.m. this Sunday!

Dogfish and Elly squealed with glee,
"we'll see our classmates, what fun this will be!"

Swimming south to Mexico, they ventured
down the coast. When they saw their
friends they cried, **"Hola amigos!"**

DOGFISH watched as his friends gathered near,
each diverse and unique, he admired EVERYONE here!

ELLY wore earmuffs, she was sensitive to loud sound.
They helped to calm her, especially in a crowd.

ANGELFISH had hearing aids, in a beautiful, bedazzled blue.

SHARK wore cool shades and had a white cane too.

CRAB always had the very best advice, his mouth
couldn't make words so he spoke on his device.

TILLY TURTLE didn't have a flipper on the right,
sassy and spirited her eyes twinkled bright.

OLLIE OCTOPUS was shy and the new kid in town.
He was good at hiding ... if he didn't want to be found!

AAC
DEVICE

"**Feliz Cumpleaños**," they all declared,
as Wally rolled out in his awesome red chair!

The group was ready for some birthday fun,
when Dogfish realized, they were **MISSING** one!

"We MUST find Ollie!" he called out with a tear.
"This party can't start unless EVERYONE'S here!"

He's a master of disguise and he's still out of sight.
Let's try his favorite foods to tempt his appetite!

They tried to coax Ollie
with yummy, scrumptious snacks,
with green plankton pizza,
and slug flapper-jacks.

Bug-a-roonie ring-a-dings,
and furry-worm cookie dough,
with sand-flea cheesy sprinkles.
But Ollie didn't show!

"Ollie loves solving puzzles,
let's give that a go!"
But NO response ...
he STILL didn't show!

We need to find Ollie
for this party to start!
Let's ask Crab for help,
he is super SMART!

They gathered around Crab
and watched as he typed.
Then everyone read,
and began to recite—

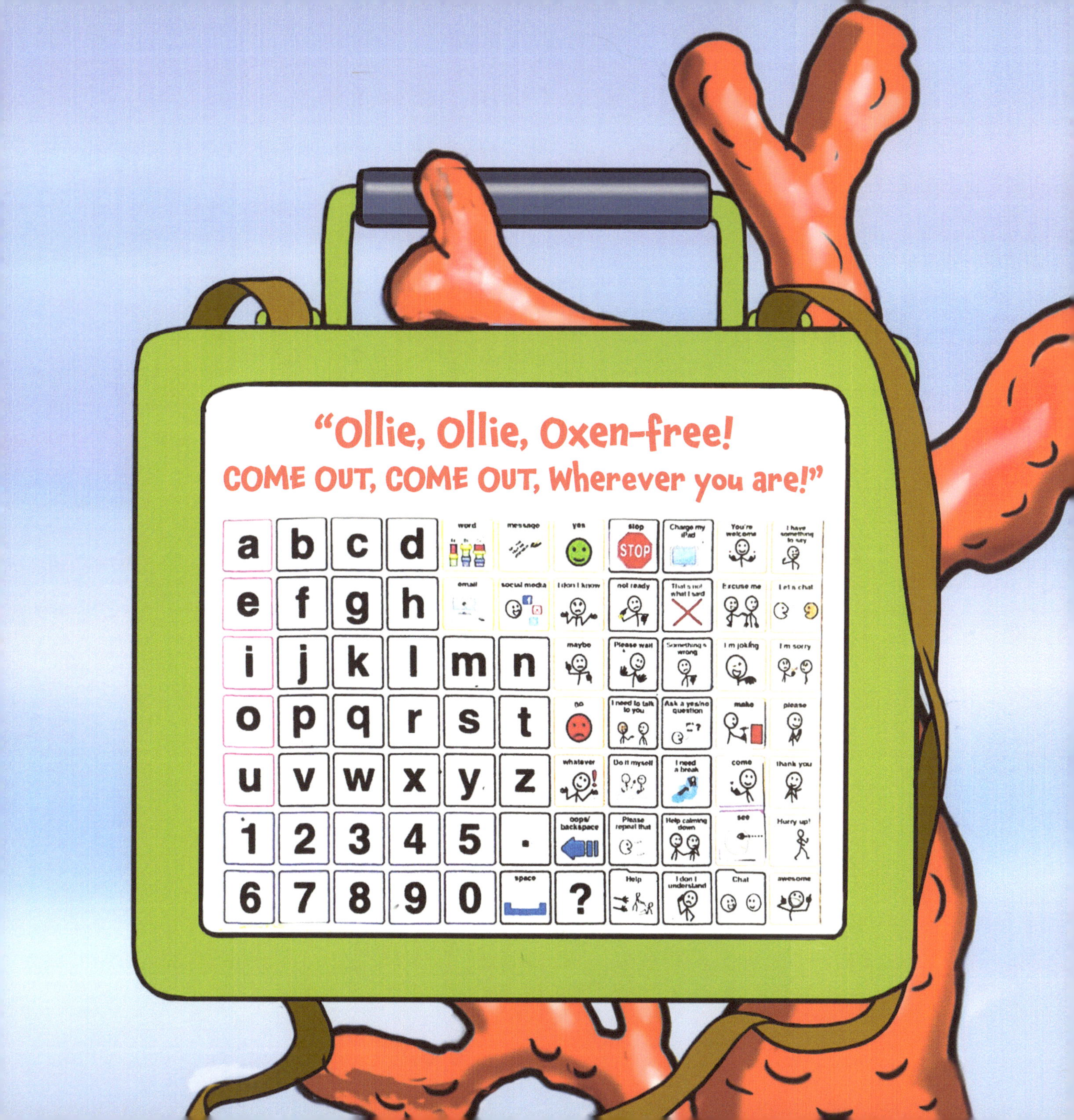
"Ollie, Ollie, Oxen-free!
COME OUT, COME OUT, Wherever you are!"

FINALLY ... Ollie appeared,
in unison they all **CHEERED!**

HAPPY BIRTHDAY

AAC DEVICE

Dogfish announced, "We have a present,
something special this year.

WE are the gift now that **EVERYONE** is here!"

TOGETHER,
we are a beautiful song,
each note is important,
we ALL belong!

Clam started with a simple sound.
He clicked and clacked
all around.

Sardines swung their tails like a pendulum.

SWISH-DA-DUM   SWISH-DA-DUM

Dogfish boogied to
the banjo beat
TRING-A-LING
TRING-A-LING

Turtle tipped and tapped
her tambourine
TING-A-TING
TING-A-TING

Come on Ollie,
you're the best at drums

BOOM-BANG
CLICKETY-CLACK
TICKETY-TING
TAP-PA-RAT-A-TAT-TAT!

The jellyfish jiggled and giggled with glee,
Their tentacles wiggled, as they kept the beat.

TOGETHER,
we are a beautiful song,
each note is important,
we ALL belong!

Together they twirled, laughed, and swayed,
EVERYONE wished Wally,

HAPPY BIRTHDAY!

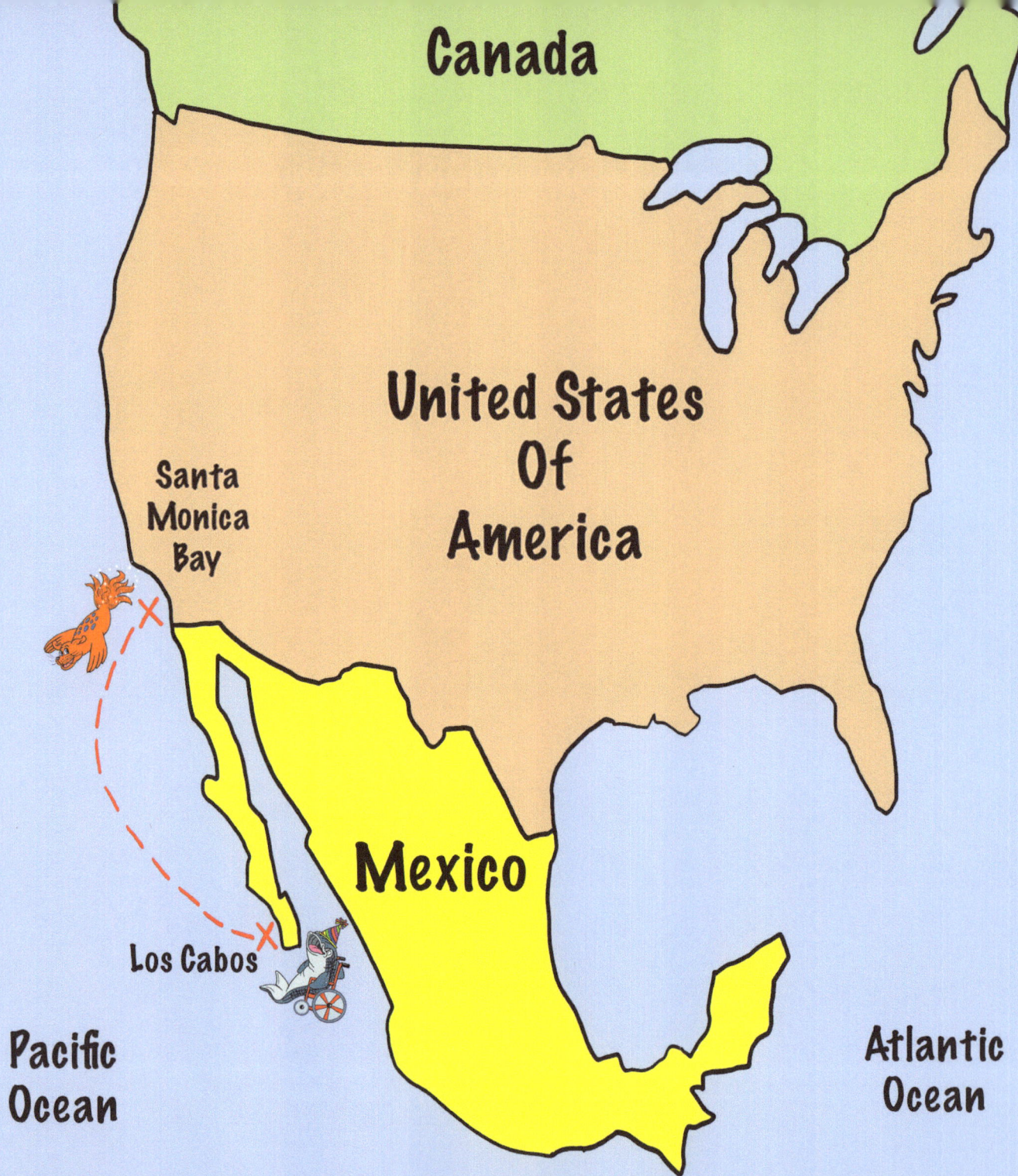

About the Author

Rita Reed lives in Southern California, where she studied art, interior design, and architecture. She enjoys spending time with her family and two silly, spoiled cats.

Rita has found extraordinary joy in creating the magical Dogfish Tales series. Through these books, she hopes to spread love, inclusiveness, positivity, and acceptance of all.

"I feel Dogfish in my heart. He's the vulnerable, innocent child in all of us."

About the Illustrator

Craig Cartwright has worked in all aspects of the visual arts world including children's books, editorial illustration, character design, and film and commercial storyboards.

His client list includes Pixar, Disney, Warner Brother (Looney Tunes), Fox (The Simpsons), The History Channel, The Family Guy, and Marvel.

Craig received a degree in commercial illustration from Commonwealth University in Virginia. He lives in Venice, California.

More Books in the Dogfish Tales Series

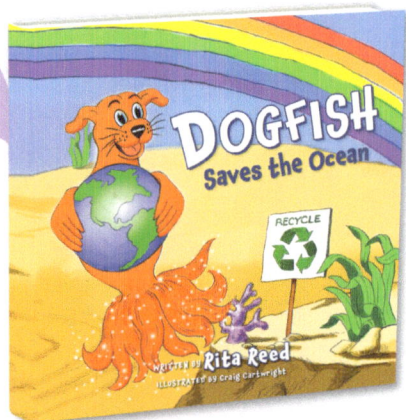

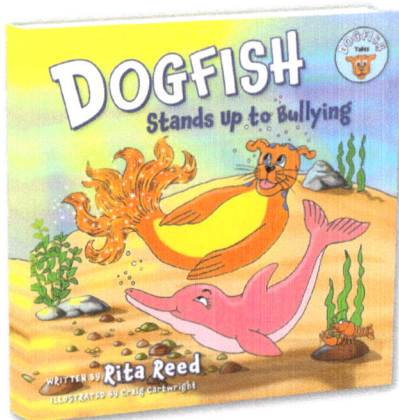

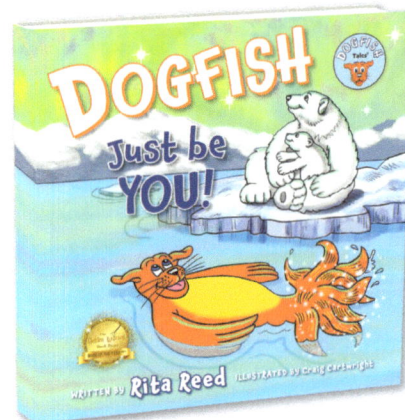

DOGFISH
Saves the Ocean
WRITTEN BY Rita Reed
ILLUSTRATED BY Craig Cartwright

DOGFISH
Stands up to Bullying
WRITTEN BY Rita Reed
ILLUSTRATED BY Craig Cartwright

DOGFISH
Just be YOU!
WRITTEN BY Rita Reed   ILLUSTRATED BY Craig Cartwright

Milton Keynes UK
Ingram Content Group UK Ltd.
UKHW021440131024
449515UK00009B/59